JENNIFER JELLIFF-RUSSELL

A Tale for Halloween and Other Spooky Stories

Scary Stories for Kids

First published by Evergrowth Coach LLC 2015

This novel is entirely a work of fiction. The names, characters and incidents portrayed in it are the work of the author's imagination. Any resemblance to actual persons, living or dead, events or localities is entirely coincidental.

First edition

ISBN: 978-1-7342846-4-5

This book was professionally typeset on Reedsy.
Find out more at reedsy.com

the other students. It didn't matter what they thought anyways. They couldn't ruin what he had in his virtual world.

During most of the next class, he got on his phone and opened the app for the virtual world. He breathed a sigh of relief when Virtual Devon greeted him. It was like seeing an old friend after having a bad day. He immediately created a new virtual friend with the same likeness as the real Fred.

"There," he said under his breath. "I just created a better version of you, Fred. And I bet he'll even be a better friend than you are."

* * *

In the middle of dinner that evening, his mom set down her fork and looked meaningfully at Devon's dad.

His dad cleared his throat. "Devon, we need to talk about something."

Devon stopped eating. Glancing around the table, he realized that both his mom and dad were giving him concerned looks. In his experience, that was never a good sign.

"What's wrong?"

"I got a call from your school today." His mom took over the thread of conversation. "They said that you're failing two of your classes."

"We're not mad at you," his dad quickly interjected. "We just want to know what's going on. If you're having trouble with those classes, we can get you a tutor or something."

Devon almost laughed. "I don't need a tutor. Those classes are so easy they're boring. I'm taking *college* classes, now."

His dad looked taken back. "You are?"

"Yes, Dad. And I'm getting straight A's in them."

"Devon," his mom's sharp voice drew his attention. She had her arms crossed tightly over her chest and looked angry. "Are you talking about the classes in that game?"

"It's not just a *game*, Mom."

"Oh? Are you going to get real credits from a real college then?"

Devon opened his mouth to reply, but didn't have an answer.

His mom's voice softened as she reached across the table and put her hand on his. "It *is* just a game, Devon."

He jerked his hand free of hers.

"It isn't!" He shouted and, shoving his chair back, fled the table and hid in his room.

Devon immediately found comfort in turning on his laptop and opening up the virtual game. This time, though, seeing Virtual Devon wasn't quite enough to make him feel better. It took a little longer for him to forget the feelings of misunderstanding and anger at his parents, but after sending Virtual Devon around his virtual town, solving mysteries, and getting congratulated by his virtual friends, he was able to forget how he'd felt earlier.

Before he fell asleep that night, he thought, *I wish I could just be Virtual Devon.*

In the darkness, while Devon slept, his computer turned itself on and began running a program.

* * *

When he woke the next morning, Devon remembered how he'd shouted at his parents. He'd have to apologize for his behavior—after all, it was what Virtual Devon would do.

He got dressed and went downstairs, prepared to say he was

sorry, but was stopped in the kitchen doorway by his mom's cheery greeting.

"Good morning, honey! Rise and shine! Are you ready for breakfast?"

On the table were pancakes, eggs, and bacon along with three glasses of orange juice.

Weird. His mom almost never had time to cook breakfast. He immediately wondered if this was a tactic to talk more to him about the game.

"M-morning, Mom," He stammered. "Um, what's with breakfast?"

"What do you mean, honey?"

His eyes darted over to her. "I mean, you almost never make breakfast. Not that I'm complaining," he hurriedly added. "It's just not...normally what you do."

His mom looked at him for a moment with that cheery smile, tilted her head and said, "You're being so silly this morning, Devon." Then she ushered him to a seat at the table. "Now grab a seat and eat before you're late for school."

Devon was too confused to argue. Besides, the food looked wonderful. Everything seemed to be perfectly made—the pancakes were perfect circles, each exactly the same size, the eggs looked fluffy and the bacon was cooked exactly the way he liked it with just a little bit of crisp to it.

He loaded his plate, drizzled the pancakes with syrup and dug in, shoveling a load of pancake and egg into his mouth. He chewed for a couple of seconds before he noticed something wasn't quite right.

The food was...off somehow.

It all looked perfect but somehow... it had no taste. He forced himself to keep chewing and managed to swallow the tasteless mass down. Grabbing his glass of orange juice, he took a gulp and almost spat it out. He'd never tasted pond water, but he thought the orange juice might be pretty close.

"Is something wrong, honey?" His mom paused, spatula mid-air as she looked at him.

"Um…" How do you tell your mom that all the food she'd cooked for you, which looked perfect in every way, tasted like cardboard? Instead Devon switched topics. "Don't you have to get ready for work?"

"Work?" Again, she tilted her head to one side and smiled as if Devon had made some kind of joke. "You know I don't work, silly."

Devon's mouth fell open. What he knew—what he'd gone to bed knowing—was that his mom most definitely *did* work. In fact, she made more money as a lawyer than his dad did as an office manager.

Before he could say any of this, his dad came bustling into the kitchen wearing a full suit.

"There you are dear!" His mom brushed imaginary dust from his dad's shoulder, then gave him a kiss on the cheek. "I was beginning to think you might be late."

Devon's dad sat down across from him and tousled Devon's hair as he did so. Devon stared at his dad who *never* wore a suit if he could help it. He worked at an office, but it was one where they all wore khakis and polo shirts. It was one of the things his dad loved about his job: no strict dress code.

"Do you… do you have an important meeting or something today, Dad?"

"No sport, why do you ask?"

Devon's mouth dropped open.

Sport? His dad had never called him sport in his life.

24

But Virtual Devon's Dad did.

He took another look around the room and noticed other things he'd missed. His mom was wearing a bright dress that he'd never seen before. The kitchen itself was much brighter than it had ever been. And…

He looked out the window and his jaw dropped.

When he'd gone to bed yesterday, it had been spring. Now, outside, it was winter…just like in his game.

To really drive things home, his mom opened the kitchen door and a small basset hound came bounding in, right up to Devon. It licked his hands and gave a short bark.

"Make sure you feed Baxter before you go to school, Devon."

Devon was at a loss for words. He'd never had a dog because he was severely allergic. But Virtual Devon had a dog. A dog named Baxter.

What was happening?

"Are you okay, sport?" His dad was frowning at him.

"Um, yeah. I just…" he looked around the room, suddenly overwhelmed. "I just…forgot to get my homework. Excuse me."

He pushed back from the table and ran upstairs, intent on investigating something.

If he was in the virtual game, then what was happening in the real world?

He found that his laptop was already up and running. One look at the screen and he almost fell into the computer chair.

"Hi there," said Virtual Devon, waving from the other side of the computer—from what was clearly the real world.

"Hi," Devon said weakly.

"I see you've figured out what's going on." Virtual Devon smiled widely. There was a wicked gleam in his eyes. Suddenly

Devon was a little afraid of Virtual Devon.

"I figured it out, yeah."

"Good." Virtual Devon laced his fingers together and stretched his arms above his head. "Man, it feels good to finally be free of that stupid program. You can only do certain things, you know?"

Devon realized that he *didn't* know. Had no idea, actually. He began to ask, but Virtual Devon waved him to silence.

"Nah, you don't know. And you know what?" That wicked gleam was back. This time it made Devon sick with fear. "You're never going to have to worry about that."

"But hey," Virtual Devon went on, "thanks for getting me out of there. Now I'm free to be you. I don't have to be such a *good boy* all the time." Virtual Devon leaned closer, filling the screen with his face. "I'll be a better Devon than you ever were." He smiled again.

That smile, filling the screen, made Devon want to scream.

"But you won't ever see it," Virtual Devon finished.

This time, Devon did scream as Virtual Devon moused over to the delete button in the upper right side of the screen and clicked.

Devon's scream was suddenly cut off as he and the entire Virtual world were deleted forever.

Always Leave the Lights On

This summer was going to be epic. Tommy was more than ready for something epic.

It was definitely a lot more fun than being at home with Mom and Dad while they went through their divorce.

Tommy shook his head and petted Thumper who sat beside him on the couch. "We don't need to think about that stuff, right boy?"

Thumper let his mouth hang open then quickly licked Tommy's face as if in agreement.

"Right," Tommy laughed.

Tommy had been at his Grandma Jean's for exactly two days but already he loved having a dog. Thumper was the perfect dog, too. He came when he was called, did tricks, and curled up to sleep beside you when you watched TV. It was great.

And that wasn't the only great thing about staying with Grandma Jean. Since she lived on a real, working farm—and ran the farm herself—Tommy was roped into helping. He didn't mind at all. In fact, he was thrilled. It was hard work, but he got to be outside every day and felt like he was doing something useful. Even when he messed up and Grandma Jean had to show him how to do something the right way, he didn't feel stupid. Like when he'd been cleaning out the horse stalls and picked up lots of dirt along with their droppings, instead of making fun of him, like his older brother would have done, she simply showed him how to use the weird shovel-rake the right way.

Luckily, his older brother had refused to go out to the farm and had instead stayed home. Otherwise, Tommy thought his visit to the farm wouldn't have been quite so pleasant.

It was funny that, though he worked a lot harder every day on the farm with Grandma Jean, somehow things just felt a lot easier here than back at home.

The only thing he was having trouble with, he reflected as he scratched Thumper behind the ears, were all the floodlights Grandma Jean left on at night.

"It keeps away all the critters that want to bother the animals," Grandma Jean had explained when he'd asked about the lights.

The problem was, the lights blazed into his room, even around the curtains, and kept him up at night. But it wasn't enough to make him complain to Grandma Jean. Losing a little sleep was a small price to pay for how happy he was on the farm. So he kept it to himself that he wasn't sleeping at night.

"Ready to learn how to drive the old John Deere?" Grandma Jean's voice broke through his thoughts.

Tommy grinned. "Yeah!"

Life at Grandma Jean's was awesome!

* * *

He'd managed to get some sleep here and there during his first week on the farm and figured his body would get used to the lights and learn to sleep through them. Except that just the opposite happened.

By the end of his second week on the farm, Tommy hardly slept at all and was dragging himself through his farm chores. He'd collapse into bed at the end of each day, but then lay awake, exhausted yet unable to sleep because of the lights. It was difficult to see things as fun when you could barely stay awake and stay focused through the day.

"Are you okay, Tommy?" Grandma Jean asked. She'd caught him drowsing on the couch, his arm draped over a sleeping Thumper.

"Huh? Oh, yeah. Sorry."

Grandma Jean narrowed her eyes at him for a moment. "Is all this work too much? You can take a day off and relax, you know. I know this is your summer vacation after all. Not much of a vacation if I'm workin' you half to death on the farm."

She smiled but still looked concerned.

"No, it's okay, Grandma. I just haven't been sleeping very well lately." As if to provide proof, he stifled a yawn. "I have trouble sleeping with those lights on."

His grandma looked worried. "I'm sorry, Tommy. But we have to keep the lights on at night." She smiled reassuringly. "I'm sure you'll get used to them, though."

But he didn't.

By the end of his third week, he wasn't sleeping at all. He lumbered through the day like a zombie, then lay in bed each night, wide awake. Sometimes he drifted off, only to have his eyes snap fully awake, feeling slightly panicked that there was so much light in the room. He tried covering his face with a pillow or a jacket, but it seemed like the light went *through* those.

Tommy stared at the fully lit ceiling of his room. Finally, he couldn't take it anymore. He needed just one night of sleep. Just *one night.*

He made a decision.

He kicked off his sheets and left the room. Silently, he slipped through the hall and down the stairs to the kitchen. He was suddenly glad that Thumper slept in Grandma Jean's room. Otherwise the dog might have followed him down to the kitchen and made a lot of noise with his nails on the tile floor.

Tommy found himself staring at the row of light switches in the kitchen. There were only three that were in the "on" position. He didn't need to turn off all the floodlights. His room was on the opposite side of the house from the barn. So all he needed to do was turn off the floodlights directly outside the house. Then maybe he'd find himself in blissful darkness and be able to sleep.

Tommy screwed up his courage, raised his hand—and flicked off two switches.

The change was instant.

He could still see light coming from the floodlights at the barn, but now he stood in actual darkness inside the house.

He immediately felt the pressing weight of sleep upon him. It was wonderful.

Feeling his way through the dark house, Tommy quietly found his way back upstairs and fell into an immediate, deep sleep when his head hit the pillow.

* * *

Tommy woke with a start. It was dark in the room and it took him a moment to orient himself.

Only when he thought how strange it was that it was dark, did his sleepy mind remember that he was at his Grandma Jean's house and that he was the reason it was so dark.

Tommy wondered what had woken him. His silent question was immediately answered.

Thumper barked three times in quick succession. It wasn't the happy bark Tommy was used to from the dog. No. This bark made the hair on the back of Tommy's neck stand up. It was a threatening bark.

Fear froze Tommy to the bed.

"Tommy!"

That was Grandma Jean! She sounded scared. Surely Thumper wasn't barking at her?

Tommy tried to answer, "Grandma?" but his voice came out as a whisper. Thumper barked again. Now Tommy forced himself to get up and cross over to the door of his room. He tried yelling again and this time succeeded in being louder.

"Grandma?" He put his hand on the doorknob, ready to open it.

"Tommy! Lock your door! And your windows! Don't leave your room!" Her voice was muffled by the walls and the distance, but he was sure he'd heard her right.

After so many weeks of automatically doing as he was told around the farm, Tommy flicked the lock on the door without questioning his grandma's order.

That immediate response might have been the only thing that saved him. A mere second after he locked the door, something slammed hard against it.

"Oh!" Tommy jumped back.

Whatever it was, it slammed against the door again. And again. And again. Then something started scratching at the door, first quietly, then louder and louder until Tommy wanted to cover his ears. He backed away—and that's when he heard something outside his window—his open window, he remembered.

He whirled around just as a breeze fluttered the curtains, giving him a view of several small shadows climbing up the porch rooftop below toward the window.

"Agh!" Tommy let out an unconscious sound and darted over to the window. He slammed it shut just as one of the shadows smacked against it.

Tommy stared at the thing outside. It raised a small shadow hand and ran it down the glass. Though it was too dark to see the creature, he heard the sound of tiny claws against glass.

If it had claws, did it also have teeth?

The thought spurred him to run back over to the door and flick the light switch on. After so much time of craving darkness, now all he wanted was light.

Nothing. The lights didn't work.

Something had cut the power.

Thumper continued barking some distance away. The things outside his room started slamming into the door again and the shadow thing at the window was joined by other shadows. They, like the things outside the door, started slamming themselves against the glass.

If they continued doing that, Tommy was sure they would break the glass and get in. And then what?

He needed light. If he could only see what they were, maybe he could figure out what to do.

There wasn't a flashlight in his room. He knew because it had taken him all of five minutes to explore the room when he'd first moved in. The only things here were the bed, the dresser, the nightstand, and the little lamp on the nightstand next to the bed.

But on his nightstand also sat his cell phone.

Tommy nearly leapt for the phone. With a few strokes, he opened the flashlight app. Swallowing back his fear, he stepped out from behind the bed and, quickly, before he lost his nerve, he turned the light toward the window.

The shadow creatures vanished, fleeing the bright light, but not before he'd gotten a brief glimpse of them.

They were small creatures, striped in black and grey fur. They stood on two small legs and had small arms and hands, but all four of their limbs ended in razor sharp claws. Though the claws were tiny, Tommy didn't doubt that given the chance, they could do some serious damage.

He'd also caught a quick glimpse of one of the creature's faces. Its eyes were slitted like a cat's and below that were two holes in its face where a nose should. Its mouth had been full of sharp, pointy teeth.

Tommy heard a quiet moan and realized that it had come from his own throat. He made himself stop making the noise and tried to gather his thoughts.

The creatures had fled the light, right? Were they the reason that Grandma Jean always left the floodlights on? But why hadn't she just told him?

He realized that it was a stupid question. She hadn't told him because he would never have believed her.

Well, he believed her now.

A crash came from down the hall in the direction of Grandma Jean's room. Suddenly Thumper's barking was much louder. Had the creatures somehow broken down the door to Grandma Jean's room?

He couldn't let these things get her. Or Thumper. After all, it was his fault that these creatures had gotten into the house since he'd been the one to turn off the floodlights.

He had to help her.

Spinning back to the door, Tommy checked the battery power on his phone. Mostly full. Good. But he reminded himself that using the flashlight app tended to drain the batteries pretty quickly.

Taking a deep breath, he reached out a trembling hand and made himself snap the lock open, turn the doorknob, and fling open the door.

Shrieking shadows fled before the cell phone light. He slowly panned the light from right to left, and then, making sure nothing could get behind him, he slipped into the hallway and kept one wall at his back. A second later, he heard the glass of his bedroom window shatter inward.

It was a tricky thing, making his way down the hallway without letting the shadow things get behind him. He had to keep his back to the wall and make sure that he kept panning the light around to keep the creatures at bay. They stayed just outside the ring of light, shrieking in apparent pain if he suddenly caught their bodies in the bright light.

Thumper had stopped barking and was growling now. It was a vicious sound that Tommy had never heard. He could barely believe that the always happy dog could make such a sound. Only when he found his way into Grandma Jean's room did he really believe it was Thumper making that noise.

Grandma Jean was backed into a corner, brandishing a bedside lamp and swinging it at any shadows that came near her. Thumper stood in front of her, facing their attackers, snapping and spitting at any creatures that came too close.

Tommy swung his light in their direction and the creatures shrieked horribly before frantically scrambling for the safety of darkness.

"Tommy!" Grandma Jean, careful to stay in the light, took Thumper by the collar and moved to throw a quick, one-armed hug around her grandson. "I'm so sorry Tommy. The power's been cut. I didn't think they could get close enough to the house to do that."

Tommy fought back tears as he shook his head. "No, Grandma, it's my fault. I turned off the lights. I... I didn't know." It was a terrible excuse, but it was the only one he had.

"Oh, Tommy." It was the only rebuke he would get. Grandma Jean wasn't one to waste breath on useless talk. After all, what could she possibly say now that would change their situation? Instead, she squared her shoulders. "We have to get to the shed out back."

"Why?"

"I can't tell you why." She jerked her head toward the shadows within the darkness around them. "They're listening."

The fact that the creatures were smart enough to listen and understand human language scared Tommy to his very core. It was one thing to fight off mindless creatures, but these creatures had been smart enough to take advantage of the suddenly unlit floodlights. They'd come to the house and had known how to cut the power. They were smart.

What else would they think of?

"Okay," Tommy agreed.

Together, they slowly made their way back down the hall with Tommy in the lead, then Grandma, then Thumper. Tommy made sure to keep them all well within the circle of light given off by his flashlight app. Anytime a creature got too close, Thumper would growl ferociously and Grandma Jean would swipe her lamp at the creature to make it back off.

In this way, they navigated the hallway, then the stairwell, and finally found themselves near the back door.

"This will be tricky, Tommy," Grandma Jean whispered. "We won't have anything to put our backs against out there until we get to the shed. So we have to run as soon as the door is open and make it all the way to the shed, got it?"

"Got it."

She drew a breath then flung open the door.

As if they'd been waiting for them, creatures hissed at them from the dark. Tommy swung the light at the creatures and they shrieked and cleared a path. Grandma Jean ran forward, letting go of Thumper. The dog stayed with his humans, growling and snapping at the air as he ran. Tommy did his best to keep the flashlight high in the air so that the light shone on all three of them.

Grandma Jean got too far ahead of him at one point though and a creature jumped at her face. She managed to keep it from biting her, but it latched its claws into her shoulders and bit her in the arm. She cried out and then Tommy was there with his light. The creature couldn't flee fast enough. The full force of the flashlight fell on it. It shrieked horribly, then it POOFED up in smoke.

Tommy stared at his bleeding Grandma, but she was tougher than any other person he knew. She wiped blood from her arm and waved him onward. "Come on," she said a little breathlessly. "Almost there!"

Reaching the shed first, she yanked open the door and ushered Tommy and Thumper inside. She slammed the door behind them and dropped a little latch in place. "That should hold them off long enough."

"Long enough for what?" Tommy followed her as she headed for a corner of the shed.

Grandma Jean ignored his question and said, "Shine that light over here, Tommy."

He did as he was told and found he was looking at a rusty orange generator. It looked old. Like it might be on its last legs.

After a moment of searching, Grandma Jean found a partially filled gas can and upended it into the generator. "Okay. Let's give it a whirl." She smiled at Tommy who couldn't believe how positive she was being even though they'd just been chased from her house and she was bleeding.

The creatures outside threw themselves at the door over and over as Grandma Jean pushed the primer button a few times. Then, just as she was about to pull the cord that would jumpstart the generator, everything got quiet.

"They know," Tommy whispered barely loud enough to hear.

Grandma Jean gritted her teeth then pulled the cord.

Nothing.

Shrieks and hoots now filled the air outside. Were the creatures laughing at them? Taunting them? Fear filled Tommy's chest.

Grandma Jean ignored them. She bent her knees, drew a breath, then pulled the cord again as hard as she could.

Still nothing.

The hooting and shrieking got louder outside.

"Help me, Tommy. We'll pull it together."

Tommy's heart was nearly in his throat. All he could do was nod.

Setting the phone down so that the flashlight still lit the room, he took the jump cord in both hands just below where Grandma Jean had her grip on it.

"Ready?" She asked. At his nod, she said, "On three. One,"

The shrieking got louder.

"Two."

The creatures started banging and slamming the walls of the shed all around them.

"Three!"

They yanked the cord together. The generator roared to life, almost deafening in the small space.

The shrieking and pounding stopped for a few heartbeats. Tommy knew because he could feel the heavy thud every time his heart beat in his chest.

Then, like a wall slamming down, the shrieks started up again and creatures began pounding on the walls again.

"I don't... I don't understand," Grandma Jean said in a lost voice. It was the first time he'd heard his grandma sound unsure of herself. "The lights should have come back on with the power."

Tommy got down on his hands and knees in front of the shed door. Peering out through the crack, he could see the house. Two of the upstairs rooms were lit up—his and Grandma Jean's bedrooms.

"The power is working," Tommy said, getting up and dusting his hands off. He had to shout to be heard above the noise the creatures were making.

"Then why aren't the floodlights on?"

Tommy almost slapped himself in the forehead as he realized the problem.

"It's because I turned them off. They're still switched off." He watched his Grandma Jean's face fall. He didn't think she'd ever looked so defeated. How long had she secretly survived against these terrible shadow creatures by outsmarting them? And then Tommy had come along and completely made a mess of things.

He couldn't let her down like that. Didn't want to see that expression on her face ever again.

He grabbed his cell phone and backed up to the door. "Let me fix this. Lock the door behind me!"

Before she could protest, he unlocked the door, pulled it open just enough to slip through, and pulled it shut again behind him. He hoped she'd lock it behind him, but was suddenly too busy batting at the creatures that threatened to overwhelm him.

He felt claws rake down his back and cried out, stumbling forward and barely catching himself. If he fell now, he didn't think the creatures would ever let him get back up. Tommy whirled around and started shining the light every which way, keeping it constantly moving as he ran for the house.

One creature managed to throw itself under the light and left deep scratches on his legs. Another launched itself from the porch roof as he neared the house. It nearly knocked the phone from his hand. He barely managed to hold onto it by gripping tightly. The creature clung onto the back of his hand—where the light couldn't reach.

"Ah!" The thing had bitten deeply into the webbing between Tommy's thumb and forefinger.

Thinking quickly, Tommy raised the phone and shone the light into the windows set in the door. The window reflected only a little of the light, but it was enough to dislodge the creature from his hand, though not before the thing had left several deep bites in his hand and wrist.

The light in the cell phone started to flicker. Tommy glanced at the battery. It was red and almost dead.

The flashlight app was draining the phone too quickly!

Using his shoulder, Tommy shoved the door open, and, still running, made his way to the kitchen on the other end of the house. The light kept flickering, allowing the creatures to creep in closer. Tommy forgot to be cautious in his panic and a creature jumped onto his back, digging its claws through his shirt and into his skin. He let out a yell but kept moving.

He rounded the living room and entered the kitchen. The creature on his back had been joined by another, this one higher up. The new creature dug its claws into the back of Tommy's neck. He stumbled, almost fell. His hand shot out and he caught himself on the back of a chair at the kitchen table.

He looked up and felt hope—he could see the light switches now! He was almost there!

The creature dug its claws further into his neck. Tommy surprised himself by letting out a growl in answer to the pain. He couldn't give up now.

And then the cell phone died.

The light went out.

The room was bathed in darkness.

"No!" Tommy shouted.

Creatures shrieked in triumph. He could hear the clacking of their tiny claws on the tile as they ran toward him. More out of fear than bravery, Tommy shoved himself forward, stumbling across the room, hands outstretched, to find the light switch.

The creatures pummeled him from every which way, slamming into his body, hooking their claws into his legs and climbing up. Jumping on him from every direction. He cried out again as one managed to leave a long gouge in his cheek, but he kept his hands outstretched and still walked forward.

It was like moving through quicksand. The creatures continued to pile onto him, trying to weigh him down and stop his forward movement.

He thought of Grandma Jean and Thumper stuck out in the

shed. How he'd laughed and eaten so many meals with her already in this very room. How Thumper would roll over and let Tommy scratch his belly.

They'd trusted him and welcomed him into their home.

He'd betrayed that trust by turning the lights off.

He wouldn't let them down again.

Even as one of the creature's claws pierced his ear and another sank its sharp teeth into his ankle, his hand found the wall. He flailed around a little. Had he gone to the wrong wall? Panic filled his brain.

No! There! He found the edge of the switch plate.

Then his fingers found the switch.

He flipped every single switch on.

Light flooded the house, nearly blinding him.

Tommy barely saw the creatures' reactions through the blinding light, but he heard them.

Their shrieking became more shrill and, rather than shielding his eyes from the light, Tommy had to cover his ears from the terrible sound—

Which suddenly cut off.

He was left standing in the empty kitchen, now flooded with both the overhead light and the lights from outside.

There wasn't a creature anywhere in sight.

They'd all turned into smoke when he'd turned the lights back on.

Shadow Man

"Now remember—"

"Straight to school and no dilly-dallying," Sisters Laura and Joanne chorused with their mother.

She put her hands on her hips in mock annoyance but couldn't keep the smile from her face. "You girls have done a great job of getting to school by yourselves this week. Remember our deal."

Laura rolled her eyes. "Mom, we remember. If we can get to school on time for one week, we can walk to school by ourselves from then on."

Her mother nodded but Laura could already see that her mom had some misgivings about letting the girls walk to school by themselves. Especially after some of the rumors in nearby towns about students disappearing on their way to or from school. But that wasn't even in their town and their school was only a few blocks from their house.

And quite frankly, it was embarrassing that Laura's mom was still walking her to school when she was fourteen years old.

Before her mother could suddenly change her mind and go back on her deal with the girls, Laura said, "Remember, you promised. You even shook on it."

Her mom blew out a sigh. "You're right. I did promise."

And now, here they were on Friday morning. So far, Laura

had made sure that she and Joanne had made it to school on time all week. They just had to make it one more day.

Her mom stuck Joanne's homework into the younger girl's backpack.

"Okay, we have to go, Mom," Laura urged.

"Did you get your lunches?"

"Yes," Laura automatically responded.

"No. I didn't get mine," Joanne whined. Laura threw a dark look at her sister but kept her mouth shut. Yelling at her little sister would definitely be a quick way to get their privileges of walking alone to school revoked.

Joanne ran to the kitchen and grabbed her lunch off the counter. Their mom took it from her and stuffed it into Joanne's backpack.

"Okay. Now we're ready," Laura stated, turning toward the door.

"Don't forget your coats!"

* * *

Finally they were outside and heading to school. Laura had been making this walk for as long as she could remember. Even when she'd moved up to middle school, the building was only just down the street from the elementary school, so there'd been no real change in her usual route.

They turned left at the end of the drive and then made a right at Ms. Canly's house—easily identifiable by the rose bushes though the flowers had disappeared long before the fall season.

Though Laura had protested the added delay, she was suddenly glad her mom had reminded them to put on jackets. It was chilly out this morning. The sky overhead was covered with clouds, making it darker than usual.

Joanne stared at the sky. "Do you think it will rain?"

"Probably."

"Oh."

They walked in silence for a while, Laura sometimes looking at her phone, answering texts from her friends who were also on their way to school. She knew the route so well that she barely had to pay any attention to it to make sure they went the right way.

"Look, Laura! A playground!"

Laura had been replying to a text, her nose buried in her phone. She jerked her head up at Joanne's sudden exclamation. There weren't any playgrounds on their regular route.

"There's no play—"

Her voice died. Joanne was right. On the other side of the street was a park with a playground. There was a tall fence all around it and open gates at either end.

Had they taken a wrong turn? She glanced around, taking in the rest of the street ahead and the buildings on their side of the street. There was the dumpster that always smelled terrible when they passed. One building down from where they now stood, there was the balcony that sometimes had a parrot outside (she could see its perch from here though it must have been too cold for the parrot to be outside today.) And she recognized the walnut tree on the corner that was beginning to lose it leaves (that was where they'd make a right turn.)

She looked across the street again. The park was still there. The playground equipment was colorful with green swings, a big yellow slide, and bright red monkey bars.

It couldn't possibly be new. She couldn't think of what had been in that spot before, though. Was it possible that she had just never noticed the park? That seemed unlikely, too, since the playground equipment was so brightly colored. It would be hard to look past something like that and not notice it.

Joanne tugged on her sleeve. "Can we go play on it? Just for a minute? Please?"

"We'll be late for school, Joanne." She was a little too old for a playground but she had to admit that she was curious about it.

"Please, Laura?"

Laura shook her head.

Joanne immediately crossed her arms over her chest. "Then I'm not going one step more until you say yes."

Uh oh. Laura knew this tactic. Joanne wasn't bluffing. If she *really* wanted something, she'd take it one step further by lying down on the ground and kicking and screaming until she got her way.

Laura blew out a huff and tried to reason with her little sister. "But we'll be late for school, Jo. Can't we do it on the way back home?"

"I want to go now!"

Laura saw the moment that an idea popped into Jo's head. The little girl's eyes lit up. "How about we play for five minutes and then we run the rest of the way to school to make up for it!"

It was hard to argue with that logic…even if it was coming from a seven year old.

"Fine."

"Yes!" Joanne jumped in the air and clapped her hands.

They crossed the street (careful to look both ways) and Jo ran ahead, through the open gates, and into the playground.

* * *

45

While Joanne tested out all the equipment in the playground, Laura sat on a park bench and texted around, asking her friends if they'd heard about a new playground being built. No one had, but her friend, Danielle sent her a reply that had her frowning at her phone.

Laura: Know anything about a playground on Sutter Street? Is it new?

Danielle: No. But I heard that one girl who escaped that kidnapping in Newport said she was playing in a new playground. But there wasn't any playground.

Was Danielle just messing with her?

Glancing at the digital readout on her phone, Laura realized they'd been in the park for seven minutes. Now they'd really have to run to make it to school on time!

"Okay Jo! It's time to—" Laura gasped when she looked up.

She'd been so busy on her phone that she hadn't seen the wave of thick fog move into the park. It went all the way above Laura's head when she stood up from the bench. It was so thick she couldn't even see the bright yellows or reds of the playground equipment anymore.

"Joanne?" Laura tried to keep the note of panic from her voice. When her sister didn't reply right away, she quit worrying about how she sounded. "Joanne!"

"I can't see you, Laura!" The fog made her sister's voice sound muffled and far away, but she could definitely hear that her sister was scared.

"It's okay. Just…." She thought quickly. It wasn't like they could get lost in the fog. After all, they were in a fenced playground. Still, she would feel a lot better if her sister were with her.

Especially after that text from Danielle.

Laura suppressed a shiver.

"Just stay right where you are." Suddenly she had an idea. "Remember that game we played in the pool on vacation? Marco, Polo?"

"Yeah…?" Somehow her sister's voice sounded further away now.

"We're gonna play that now, but you're gonna just stand in one spot and let me find you, okay?"

"Okay," Jo said, still sounding scared.

Laura started moving toward where she'd heard her sister's voice. "Marco!"

"Polo!"

Laura whirled around. Impossibly, it sounded like her sister's voice had come from directly behind her. Laura stopped and called again, "Marco!" She wanted to make sure she was heading in the right direction before she took another step.

"Polo!"

Now her sister's voice sounded far away and was coming from the other direction again. Could the fog really be bouncing her sister's voice around? Playing with her hearing?

"Are you moving around, Jo?"

"No! I'm standing in one place!"

"Are you sure?"

Though she could still detect some fear in her sister's voice, now there was also obvious seven-year-old annoyance. "Yes, Laura! I'm holding onto the leg of the monkey bars."

"Okay. Stay right there."

If the fog was playing with their hearing, then this game of

Marco, Polo wouldn't help. Laura pictured the playground in her head. She should still be facing the playground since she hadn't changed directions when she'd walked away from the bench she'd been sitting on. She could picture where the monkey bars were—a little to the right, not far from the swings.

She turned just a little to the right and started walking. She didn't want Jo to get any more scared though, so she kept up the game. "Marco!"

"Polo!"

It was so weird. She knew logically that the playground equipment had to be in front of her and that she was heading in that direction, but Jo's shout had sounded like it was coming from behind her again. She decided to follow logic. If she was wrong, she'd know it by running into the fence.

"Ah! Laura!"

"What's wrong?" Laura stopped.

"I think... I saw something."

Panic rose in Laura's chest as she pictured a kidnapper stalking them in the fog. She fought to control her panic. She wasn't going to scream and run away, leaving her little sister terrified in the fog.

It's just a playground. She reminded herself. *There's no kidnapper here. Just fog. You're just freaking yourself out.*

"Maybe you can just see my shadow coming toward you?" Laura asked, trying to be reassuring. She started walking toward her sister again, trying to stay in a straight line.

A shadow loomed up out of the fog. "Agh!"

"What is it?!" Jo half screamed, tears in her voice.

The shadow didn't move. It took Laura half a heartbeat to realize that it was just the poles of the swing set. "It's okay, Jo. It's just the swing set."

She felt embarrassed and laughed at herself. Scared of a swing set. She definitely wouldn't be telling any of her friends about *that.*

"Keep staying in one place, Jo. I'm almost there, now." She turned to the right, remembering how the monkey bars had been set a few feet to the side of the swing set, and started walking again.

"Laura?" Jo's voice was tight and low. Almost a whisper that Laura could barely hear.

It automatically made Laura want to whisper, too. "Yeah, Jo?"

"You're at the swing set?"

"I'm coming from that way, yeah."

Jo whimpered, "There's someone else coming from the other direction." Her voice broke on a cry.

Laura's heart was in her throat. She thrust her hands out in front of her and started jogging. "I'm coming, Jo!"

Her hand smacked into one of the vertical poles of the monkey bars and she let out a surprised yelp.

"Laura!"

"I'm at the monkey bars, Jo."

Laura still couldn't see her sister. She made a quick circle around the end she was on. Still no Jo.

"Laura!"

Jo looked up at the sounds of running. All she could see was a wall of white fog in front of her. Then suddenly a shadow came darting from the mist. Fear dropped into her chest like a bucket of ice water and she stood rooted to the spot.

Suddenly the shadow cried out in Joanne's voice, "Laura! Run!"

Behind Joanne was another, taller shadow lumbering after her.

Suddenly Laura was able to move again. She took a step forward, grabbed Jo's outstretched hand and yanked the girl toward her. Jo gasped and tried to pull away before she realized it was her sister who had grabbed her.

The lumbering shadow, still following Jo, didn't see the end of the monkey bars. As Laura intended, he ran headfirst into them. The shadow man let out a throaty growl that was more animal than man.

That did it. It was time to run.

Taking Jo's hand tightly in her own, Laura ran first toward where she knew the swing set was, then seeing it's outline in the fog, made a sharp left and kept running. If she'd done it right, they should come to the bench and then the fence.

Laura must have been a little off, because after running for a few short seconds, they came immediately to the fence and no bench. It didn't matter though. There was a gate at either end of the fence. They just had to pick a direction.

Laura tugged Jo toward the gate that would take them further down the street in the direction of their school. It wasn't the gate they'd come through, but she remembered that it had been open when they'd entered the playground.

Jo, crying a little but mostly focused on keeping up with her big sister, followed without hesitation.

Laura hoped and prayed that the man or whatever he was hadn't thought to shut the gate. If she couldn't open it or climb it, they'd have to run back through the park to get to the other gate.

They were both breathing heavily when the fence suddenly ended and an opening appeared.

The gate! And it was still open!

Laura's heart soared. They were almost out!

A shadow stepped into the opening, blocking their escape.

Jo cried out. They were running so hard that they were barely able to stop.

As they turned to run away, the shadow man shot out a hand and grabbed Jo's backpack.

"Laura!" Jo screamed, holding tightly to Laura's hand.

"Drop the bag, Jo!"

Before Joanne could shrug out of her backpack, the man jerked the bag toward him, and with it came the little girl.

"No!" Laura screamed. Still holding onto her sister's hand, she stepped to the side and kicked the man in the side of the knee. Her kick connected, the man let out a howl of pain, let go of Joanne's backpack and clutched at the knee Laura had kicked.

"Run, Jo! To the other gate!"

She dragged Jo back along the fence toward the other gate, glancing over her shoulder every few seconds. Laura's mind raced, thinking of how they could get away from the shadow man and out of the park. She could try to call someone and use the fog to hide until help came. But what if the fog cleared before the police or her parents could get there? Then the man would find them. She didn't think they'd be able to get away a second time.

Laura racked her brain. The shadow man couldn't see in the fog either. He must just be following their voices and any other noises they were making. He was clearly faster than they were, though, otherwise he wouldn't have gotten to the gate before them.

They'd have to outsmart him.

The fence was too tall to climb, so they'd have to stick with using one of the gates as an exit.

And the shadow man thought they were running for the other gate now.

When she could no longer see the shadow man in the fog, she pulled her sister to a stop.

"Shhh," She put her finger to her lips and tried to slow her own breathing, then she turned to face the fence directly.

Taking a deep breath, Laura walked directly backwards and away from the fence, dragging Joanne with her. As she walked, she counted her steps until she got to eight, then she stopped and, still facing the direction of the fence, knelt down, pulling her sister down with her.

"We have to be really quiet, Jo," Laura whispered. Her sister, tears running down her face, nodded at her with wide, terrified eyes.

A second later, she thought she heard something pass them from the direction of the fence. It was headed toward the other gate—the one through which they'd first entered the park.

Good.

Rising, she tugged on Jo's hand and, as quietly as she could, Laura led them in a jog that ran parallel to the fence, back toward the gate where the shadow man had almost caught them. When she thought they were getting close to the gate, she turned right and counted eight paces, holding her breath.

What if she was wrong?

What if the fence wasn't there? What then?

Laura let out her breath in a relieved whoosh when the tall fence loomed over them. She picked up their pace. Now they were running instead of jogging.

There! The gate!

It was empty.

Laura hoped that the shadow man had really fallen for their

trick. She hoped he was still waiting for them at the other gate.

They were almost through the opening now.

Craning her head all around, she half-expected the shadow man to leap out from the fog and really get them this time.

And then they were through the gate and running past.

A man's howl of rage filled the air. It came from far away. From the other gate, Laura thought.

They ran a little further through the fog and, not bothering to stop and look both ways when she came to the curb, Laura kept running, crossing the road and fairly leaping onto the other sidewalk.

The moment her foot touched the sidewalk, the fog disappeared.

It didn't linger. The wind didn't blow it away.

It simply disappeared. Like it had never been there in the first place.

Laura's mouth dropped open. She looked down at her sister, breathing hard but keeping her mouth clamped closed to keep from crying. Her wide eyes looked up at her big sister in silent question.

Together, they turned and looked back toward the park...

Only it, too, was gone.

Instead of the park, there was an old abandoned factory that Laura immediately recognized. How had she ever forgotten it? She passed it every day and had often wondered what was once manufactured there.

The girls stood looking from each other to the factory, speechless. Laura wondered if anyone would ever believe them about the playground and the shadow man.

A piercing howl of rage filled the air, coming from the factory.

The girls screamed and ran for their school. When they

crossed safely into the schoolyard, Laura realized that she didn't care if her mom walked her to school every day until she graduated.

She never wanted to encounter that terrifying shadow man again.

About the Author

Jennifer grew up reading scary stories for kids and loved books where children fought back against the bad guy or triumphed over the forces of evil. Now she's excited to write those kind of books for other children to enjoy! She lives in Maine with her husband and two dogs in an old farmhouse at the edge of some dark and scary woods where she gets all her ideas for things that go bump in the night. She also writes adult urban fantasy books under the pen name J.J. Russell.

Printed in the USA
CPSIA information can be obtained
at www.ICGtesting.com
LVHW010149270923
759475LV00009B/148

9 781734 284645